Blimey, That's Slimy!

Barnacle Barb & Her Pirate Crew

Written by Nadia Higgins
Illustrated by Jimmy Holder

magic wagon

For Henry and Harold, who teach me all about ocean life

visit us at www.abdopublishing.com

Published by Magic Wagon, a division of the ABDO Publishing Group, 8000 West 78th Street, Edina, Minnesota 55439.

Printed in the United States.

Text by Nadia Higgins
Illustrations by Jimmy Holder
Edited by Bob Temple
Interior layout and design by Emily Love
Cover design by Emily Love

Library of Congress Cataloging-in-Publication Data
Higgins, Nadia.
 Blimey, that's slimy! / Nadia Higgins ; illustrated by Jimmy Holder.
   p. cm. — (Barnacle Barb & her pirate crew)
 ISBN 978-1-60270-091-8
 [1. Pirates—Fiction. 2. Practical jokes--Fiction.] I. Holder, Jimmy, ill. II. Title. III. Title: Blimey, that is slimy!
PZ7.H5349558Bl 2008
[E]—dc22
                            2007036974

The deck was swabbed. The parrot was fed. The treasure was polished and stacked.

His chores done, Slimebeard took a deep breath of the warm, salty air. "Mmmmmmm," he said, "a perfect afternoon to catch me winks." With that, the pirate curled up on a pile of sails and drifted off to sleep.

It was the moment Armpit Arnie had been waiting for. "Tee-hee-hee," he giggled. He tiptoed up to his snoring friend and got to work.

Just then Stinkin' Jim strolled by.

"Shiver me timbers! What are—?" Stinkin' said.

"Shhhhh!" Armpit hissed. "Don't wake him up! This is going to be the best pirat-ical joke ever!"

"Ta-da!" Armpit Arnie said when he was done.

Slimebeard's black, greasy beard didn't look like a wild octopus anymore. It was tied up in six neat braids. At the end of each braid was a firecracker ready to pop.

"Oh, Armpit, 'tis a masterpiece!" Stinkin' said.

"Get ready for the surprise of yer life, me little Sleepin' Brute-y," Armpit whispered. "Three, two, one—"

Pop! Pop, pop, POP! BANG-edy-bang, bang, bang!

"Attack! Attack!" Slimebeard screamed.

Barnacle Barb, Pegleg Pedro, and Shrimp-Breath Sherman rushed on deck, waving their swords in the air. But they soon saw the cause of the ruckus.

"Pfffffft, yech, BLECH." Slimebeard was a hopping cloud of smoke that spat and sputtered around them.

"Looks like Armpit's been up to his old pranks again," Barnacle Barb said. "Ye can put your swords away."

When the smoke cleared, even Armpit Arnie gasped at the sight.

"Me beard!" Slimebeard shrieked. He clawed at his chin. "Me be-he-he-he-ard!"

Everyone knew that the pirate's slimy beard was his greatest pride. Each day, he carefully groomed it, rubbing the greasy tresses with a secret concoction of goo. No one but Slimebeard knew which ingredients were mixed from the hundreds of bottles in the pirate's slime collection.

But now Slimebeard's beard was a frizzy heap of tangles! It was as frayed as old rope and drier than sun-scorched sand.

Slimebeard instantly knew who was to blame. "ARRRRRRRMPIT!" Slimebeard wailed, leaping at the practical joker. Armpit dove behind a giant vat of blubber, but Slimebeard managed to grab him by the ankle.

"Ye lower-than-plankton little . . . ," Slimebeard sputtered. Armpit squirmed like a worm on a hook. But he could not break free of Slimebeard's angry grip. Slimebeard lifted Armpit over his head and spun him around.

Slimebeard spun Armpit right into the vat of blubber. Then, he picked up a cannonball in each hand. *Bong!* He clapped them together under Armpit's chin.

"Aaaaye!" Armpit Arnie screamed, his ears buzzing like a swarm of flies. He hopped out of the vat and tried to run away.

"Get me grape soda!" Slimebeard barked. Shrimp-Breath Sherman handed him a jug right away.

As Slimebeard chugged, the other pirates clapped and hollered with delight.

"Looks like Armpit's gettin' a purple burple!" Pegleg Pedro cheered.

BUUUUUURRRRRRRP! Slimebeard's belch rang out over the sea. Its windy force pinned Armpit Arnie against the ship's rails.

In one final move, Slimebeard grabbed a ladder. "Take that, ye flounder-faced scallywag!" he said, slamming the ladder over Armpit Arnie's head.

The pirates stood, waiting for the familiar *crash*. But there was no *crash*— only a *swoosh*. Armpit Arnie had slipped between the rungs. There he stood, completely stuck. The ladder spread out from his sides like a giant, wooden tutu.

The pirates pulled on Armpit. They twisted him. They jiggled and shook him. But nothing could free the unhappy pirate.

"Slimebeard," Barb said, "we need slime from yer slime collection. If Armpit be slippery, he may unstick."

But Slimebeard refused. "Serves him right," he huffed, scratching his fried beard.

That night, Armpit Arnie couldn't get into his hammock. So, he tried to sleep leaning against a mast.

"Have a heart, me hearty," Barnacle Barb said to Slimebeard the next day. Armpit looked like he had half-empty treasure bags drooping from his eyes.

"Arrrrgh," Slimebeard sighed. "Maybe just *one* dose from me slime cellar."

Slimebeard's slime cellar was deep in the hold of the ship. There, locked behind heavy, wooden doors, lay the pirate's dearest treasure. Inside, rows of shelves held bottles of every shape and kind. Each bottle had a label describing its precious contents.

Slimebeard scanned the labels: "Jellyfish guts, oak-cured, aged ten years," he murmured. "Mashed sea slugs, 1743. Piranha pus from the South Seas." As if in a trance, the pirate reviewed his collection.

At last he returned with a bottle labeled, "Not-so-special, just-regular algae."

"Apply one capful three times a day," he instructed. Then he left to groom his beard. Barnacle Barb carefully followed Slimebeard's directions, but the algae didn't work.

The next day, Armpit Arnie tried turning around.

"That ladder bonked me right in the belly!" Barb complained to Slimebeard. She showed him the bruise. "Slimebeard, we need something stronger!" Slimebeard stroked his beard. It felt much better already.

"Arrrgh, OK," he sighed. This time he came back with a bottle labeled, "Clam drool, 1643."

"Apply as needed," he said, returning to tend to his beard. Barb slathered Armpit, but the ladder wouldn't budge.

The next day, the pirates played in their dodge-cannonball league. But without Armpit Arnie—their best player—they lost the game.

The disappointed crew begged Slimebeard.

"We need stronger slime!" Stinkin' Jim said.

"The strongest slime in the sea!" said Pegleg Pedro.

"In all the seas!" Shrimp-Breath Sherman said.

"In the world!" Barnacle Barb cried.

"Slimebeard," Armpit pleaded, "I need the best slime in the history of pirates!"

Slimebeard looked at his disappointed friends. He knew what he had to do.

"Stand back!" he ordered.

Slimebeard marched up to Armpit Arnie. He took his beard in two hands. Slowly, he began to twist.

"He's wringing his beard!" Barnacle Barb gasped.

As Slimebeard wrung, a single drop began to form at the beard's end. The pirates stood spellbound by the amazing liquid. It was the most-oozy, gooey, drooly, moldy, muddy, snotty drop they had ever seen.

For a moment, the magical drop dangled on the tip of the beard. Then, with the slightest *plop*, it splashed onto the ladder.

Whoooosh. The ladder slipped off Armpit Arnie. It banged on the deck, taking Armpit's pants with it.

"Blimey, that's slimy!" Armpit yelped.

Armpit pulled up his pants and stepped over the ladder.

"Slimebeard," he said, slapping his friend's back, "yer a lard-faced scallop-butt, but I'm glad yer beard be alright."

"Armpit Arnie," Slimebeard replied, "yer an overgrown sea cucumber, but I'm glad that ladder let you go."

"Who's up for a game of dodge-cannonball?" Pegleg Pedro called out.

"I am! I am!" each pirate shouted. And soon the pirates were winging cannonballs at each other's heads.

"Arrrrrgh," Barnacle Barb sighed, looking with satisfaction at her crew. "'Tis so lovely when all the mates get along."

Pirate Booty

The most famous, fiercest pirate was Blackbeard. A British pirate, Blackbeard terrorized the Carolina and Virginia colonies in the early 1700s. Blackbeard was known for his fearsome looks. His wild beard was braided into long, black strands that stuck out in all directions. During battle, he was known to put long, lighted matches under his hat. That way, his face and wild beard would appear to be circled in fire and smoke. To his enemies, Blackbeard looked like the devil himself.

Pirate Translations

blimey — wow
catch me winks — take a nap
me hearty — my friend
scallywag — rascal
shiver me timbers — oh, my
swab the deck — mop the deck